This book is dedicated to
Albert Einstein, Nikola Tesla, Steve Jobs
and Ross Allen

Manufactured in the USA.
The text of this book is set in Coming Soon, Just Me Down
Here and Minion Pro. The illustrations are watercolor,
pencil and ink paintings reproduced in full color.

Book design by Sunghee Lee

StarField Stories, Inc.
www.starfieldstories.com

ISBN-10: 1500688282
ISBN-13: 978-1500688288

# Crusty Bigglebones

Written and illustrated by LORD TOPH

StarField Stories

Crusty was a boy like a few boys
I've met in my day.

Crusty really never liked going outside...
and very rarely would Crusty ever think
about going out to play.

Crusty loved to watch TV. in fact, he watched it all the time!

He'd snack while watching his favorite shows, but
most were filled with violence and crime!

"Turn that off!" his mother
would yell.
"Go find something else to do."

"Alright alright!"

Crusty would mumble, before
going to his room.

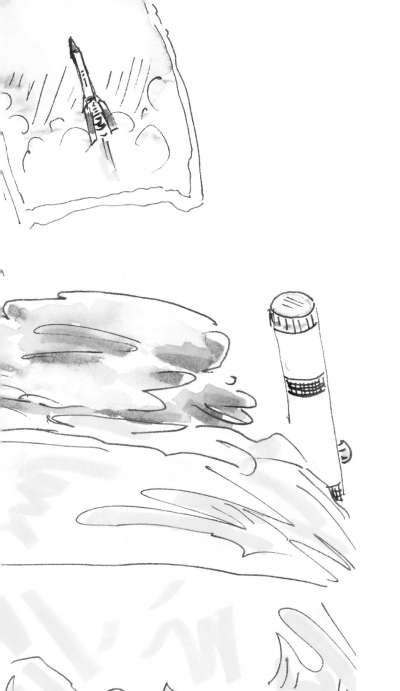

There he felt most comfortable, in his pig sty of a mess.

Crusty would fiddle, foddle, faddle, and fix... which is really what he did best.

He had a keen understanding
for things.

But surprisingly, he didn't do so
well in school.

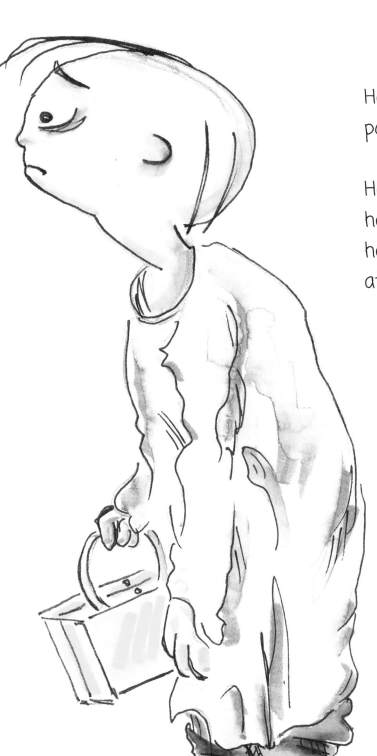

He just never was too
popular among his peers.

He wasn't neat,
he wouldn't study,
he wasn't funny,
athletic or cool.

Actually, his messiness is why most other kids stayed away.

His hygiene wasn't quite up to par... it even kept peoples' pets at bay!

One fine day seemed to come along, when Crusty would invent...
something so very neat, clever, and original...
it impressed the president!

The President said eagerly,

"This kid has come up with a way to travel into space and do it in a bubble.

He's even made it without any special training and without getting into trouble!"

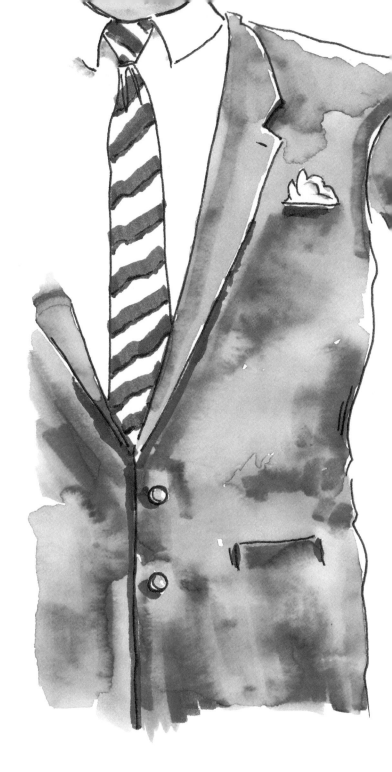

When Crusty ended up
finally being on TV instead
of always watching...

He instantly became so busy, famous,
and all cleaned up...
that there was never time for stopping.

"What will you do next?" a reporter asked.
"Are there any plans that you have soon?"

Crusty's fans giggled when he chuckled.

Then he answered, "I'll be traveling to the moon!"

"Then, I'll visit other planets to
see if there is life out there."

A regular Einstein Crusty
became, and his stories he
would share... about all kinds of
beings out there in space that
were kind to him in his travels...
with mysteries of the universe,
and how it all unravels.

So let the moral of this story be... like one that will make history.

Let's not judge a book by its cover, before we even learn to read.

A true lesson learned is a story... like the story of Crusty Bigglebones, indeed!

# More books by Lord Toph

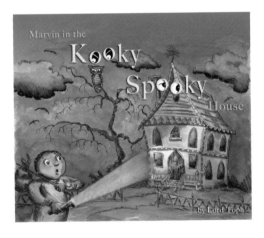

## Fuzzy McKenzie

*Fuzzy McKenzie* is a humorously delightful story about a lively little girl, and how a mishap on a rainy day led to happiness that could chase the clouds away.

## Marvin in the Kooky Spooky House

Only a few days before Halloween, and young Marvin, is already in for a big scare.
So when the time is right, he strikes out late in the night, to visit that spooky house up there.
You're in for a treat when you read to find out how Marvin gets tricked out of being frightened, once he bravely enters the Kooky Spooky House!

For more information about Lord Toph's books, please visit us at

www.starfieldstories.com

# About the Author

Lord Toph was born in Little Rock, Arkansas, and has resided in New York for several years. He wrote his first story entitled, "The Fing" at the mere age of seven. He has written and illustrated well over thirty children's stories since this tender age. As head of his own multimedia company (Monté CrisToph Multimedia), Lord Toph produces performing artists and creative concepts ranging from fine art to music and literature.

He is an artist, composer, producer, and writer. He has written several volumes of poetry, as well as works in short story and novel length.

Bruce County Public Library
1243 Mackenzie Rd.
Port Elgin ON N0H 2C6

CPSIA information can be obtained at www.ICGtesting.com
Printed in the USA
LVIW01n1749301014
411272LV00008B/94

\* 9 7 8 1 5 0 0 6 8 8 2 8 8 \*